"The Royal Duck and Duckess are very kind," Mother Duck told her children. "They always give us breakfast. See how they walk like us with their wings folded behind them."

TUFTY

The Little Lost Duck who Found Love

Michael Foreman

ANDERSEN PRESS

A family of ducks lived on an island in the middle of a lake.
At the edge of the lake there was a beautiful palace and a park.
Each morning the ducklings paddled along behind their mother.
The youngest, Tufty, always struggled to keep up.

Some evenings, Tufty and the other ducks
watched the Duck and Duckess dance at
grand parties under great crystal chandeliers.

As the golden summer passed, the nights grew
colder and the ducklings cuddled closer.

"Soon, we will have to fly south where the winter is warmer,"
said Father Duck, "so practise your flying, little ducks."

One day, Father Duck said, "Time to go!" And off they flew,
up and away from the lake, and the palace and park.

Tufty was amazed to see that all around the park was a huge city. Roads and railways criss-crossed between towering buildings that seemed to touch the cloudy sky.

Poor Tufty struggled to keep up with the other ducks. The tall buildings made it even more difficult and soon he lost sight of his family.

He flew on, growing more tired and lost. Then it began to rain and get dark. "I must find a safe place to rest," he thought. Suddenly he saw what looked like an island amongst the traffic.

Tufty landed safely, but the noise of the roaring traffic all around was frightening. Exhausted, he took shelter in a tunnel leading down under the island.

A man was sitting in the quiet tunnel.
"Hello, little one," he said. "This isn't a good
place for a duck. Here, have something to eat,
then we will find a better place for you."

The man shared his food with Tufty
and then scooped him up into his
arms. "Let's go, little one."

They left the
thundering traffic
behind them and came
to a dark wood next to a
small lake. The man moved
some branches from the foot of
a chestnut tree. "Welcome to my
home, little one," he said.

Tufty saw that the tree was
hollow, and inside was dry
with a bed of straw.
Feeling tired but safe he
fell asleep in the man's hat.

Tufty woke to the wonderful smell of cooking. Pigeons cooed in the tree and a family of squirrels waited for a share of the man's breakfast. The quiet lake was covered in mist.

After breakfast Tufty got ready for the lonely flight south. But the mist still hid the tops of the trees and Tufty knew he would never find his way on his own.

So he spent the winter sleeping in the man's hat, sharing his meals and slowly growing bigger and stronger.

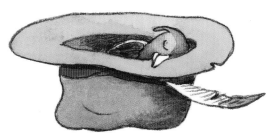

In the springtime, as the days grew warmer, Tufty saw flocks of ducks flying overhead. His family was returning to the lake beside the palace. Tufty flew up to join them.

Together they flew back to the palace gardens.
Each day, more and more ducks arrived at the lake.

Tufty noticed a little brown duck. He thought
he had never seen anyone more beautiful.
"Let's get away from the crowd," he said to her
one day. "Let's spread our wings and fly away."

Together, they flew to the lake in the woods.
Trees were bursting into blossom and the chestnut
tree was more beautiful than any chandelier.

"Just in time for tea," smiled the man.
"Welcome home."

Bogtrotter lived in a gloomy
cave in a marshy, mushy bog.
Every morning he stretched,
yawning and blinking,
outside his cave.

Then
he started
running.

He ran across
the bog,
up the bog,

BOGTROTTER

Margaret Wild

Illustrated by Judith Rossell

WALKER BOOKS
AND SUBSIDIARIES
LONDON • BOSTON • SYDNEY • AUCKLAND

down
the
bog

and around
the bog until it
was time to go home.

He ran day after day,
week after week,
year after year.

Sometimes he felt bored,
but he didn't know why.

Sometimes he felt lonely,
but he didn't know why.

Sometimes he wished things would change,
but he didn't know how or what or why.

One afternoon, a frog said,
"Why do you run all day long?"

Bogtrotter stopped.

"Because that's what Bogtrotters do,"
he said.

"Don't you ever do anything new and different?"
asked the frog.

"No," said Bogtrotter.

"Ah," said the frog, and away it hopped.

Bogtrotter stared
after the frog.
He sighed.
He shuffled
his feet. Poking
between his toes
was a pretty
yellow flower.

For the first time in his life, he picked a flower.

He smelled it.

He twirled it.

He stuck it behind
his ear.

"Ah," said Bogtrotter.
Then off he ran.

That night in his boggy bed,
Bogtrotter went to sleep
holding the flower,
his heart hopeful.

The next morning Bogtrotter
went running as usual.
But he made himself stop
to make friends with
a family of muskrats.

The morning after that
he stopped to swing
from a tree.

And the morning after that he stopped
to make a daisy chain of tiny pink flowers.
"Ah," said Bogtrotter.

From then on, Bogtrotter still kept on running.
Because that's what Bogtrotters do.
But every now and again,
he stopped to do something
new and different.

He stopped to splash about
with a family of ducks.

He stopped to dance
in the summer rain.

He stopped to slide down
a slippery bank.

And he hurried
back to fill his home
with bulrushes
and waterlilies.

He should have been happy,
but he wanted something more.
He just didn't know what or
who or why.

One morning, he saw the frog again.

"Do you ever run outside the bog?" the frog asked.

"No," said Bogtrotter.

"Why not?" asked the frog.

"I don't know," said Bogtrotter.

"Ah," said the frog, and away it hopped.

Bogtrotter stared after the frog. He sighed.

He stared at the flat green line of the bog
where it met the huge, blue sky.

Off he ran, as usual. But for the first time in his life, he stopped at the uttermost edge of the bog.

Taking a deep breath,
he climbed over a rotten log.

He scrambled up
a grassy bank.

He clambered over
an old stone wall.

"Ah," said Bogtrotter.

And he started running.

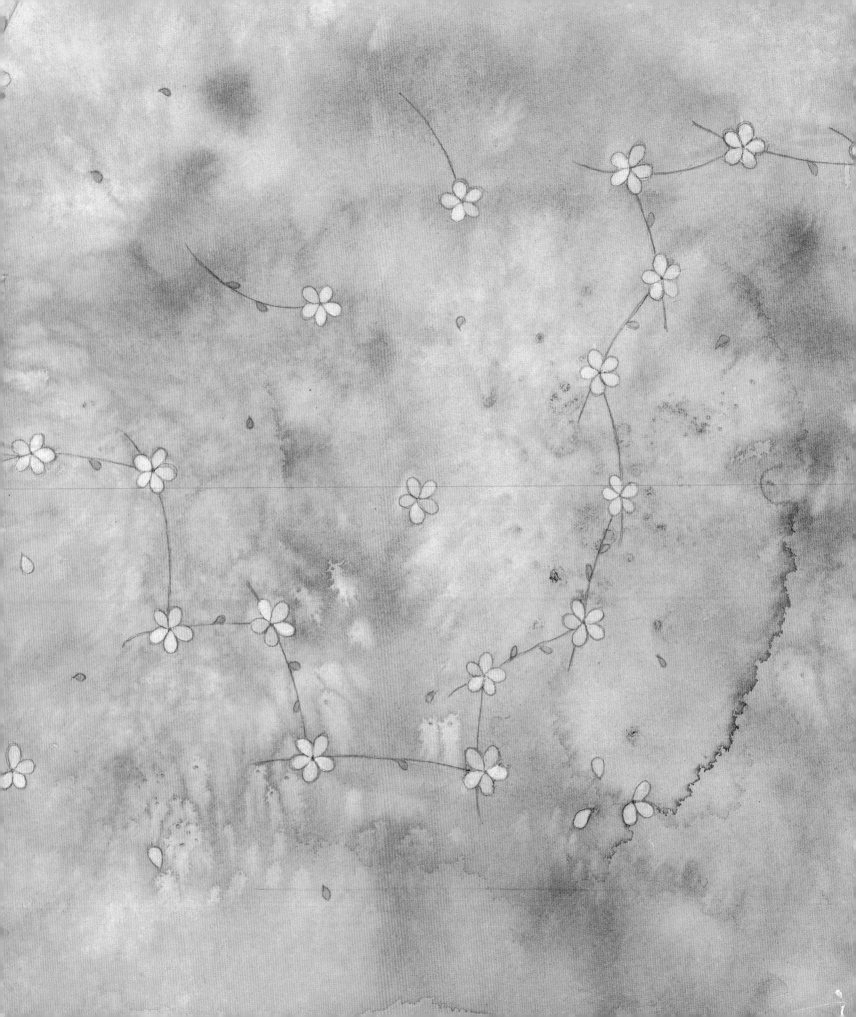

be sure to choose your pet wisely.

(And remember they are
choosing you too.)

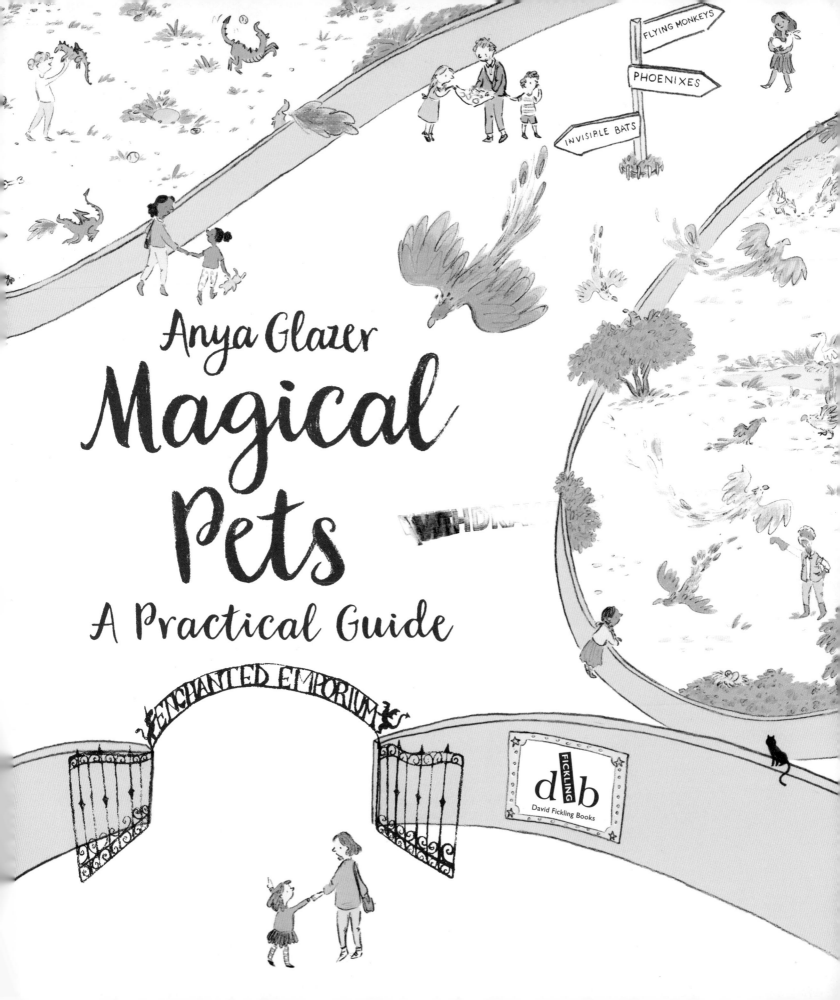

Anya Glazer

Magical Pets

A Practical Guide

FLYING MONKEYS

PHOENIXES

INVISIBLE BATS

ENCHANTED EMPORIUM

db
FICKLING
David Fickling Books

First things first . . .

Some pets will be harder work

ribbit?

than others . . .

. . . and some will be harder work
than most!

So, you will have to teach them some discipline.

sit!

uh-oh!

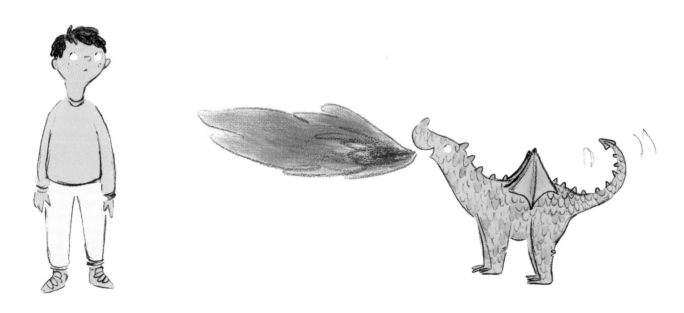

You might even be able to

teach them a few tricks.

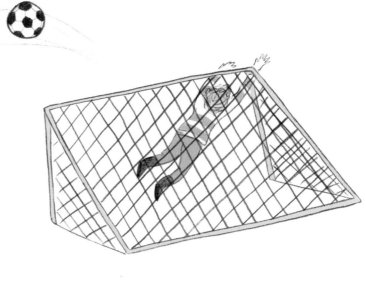

They'll need lots of exercise . . .

KEEP OFF
THE GRASS

. . . and plenty to eat.

Sometimes looking after your magical pet

can be pretty tough . . .

pssht

Swoosh

. . . but it will also be the most fun.

Ooooh

hoot hoot

They will be

your

Mmmmmmm

aaaahhh

VERY

best

friend . . .

. . . and they will never stop surprising you.